W9-DEG-155

BEAR
AGAINST
TIME

Jean-Luc Fromental · Joëlle Jolivet

NORTON YOUNG READERS
An Imprint of W. W. Norton & Company
Independent Publishers Since 1923

Bear has a heart of gold, but he sleeps a lot.
At **7 o'clock**, he lifts up his head—
but goes right back to sleep.

At **8 o'clock** he cries,
"Quick! Breakfast! Toast! Butter! Honey!

"Too late,"
sighs Mom.
"Get going . . .

. . . and don't forget to wash!"

8:15, time for the bus!

Too bad for bear.

When you're late, you're late.

Every morning, it's the same.
If he carries on like this,
Bear will never learn how to read,
count, or write.

At recess, he's all alone in the empty classroom.

Lunch is at noon, not **1:00**.

Music is at **2:00**.
Bear is ready . . .

. . . for gym.

3:00, the bell has rung, school is over.

Bear will have to walk.

At **8 o'clock** in the evening, Bear is still not home. Everyone is worried.

Dad is frantic.
"Where on earth did he go?"

Mom says, "It seems he's at the police station!"

"This bear has stolen
a whole lot of pastries,"
says the officer.

"Of course," says
my sister. "He didn't
eat all day."

My parents have to pay for
the meringues, éclairs, and tarts.

"If you do that again,
we will not be able to
keep you."

"I was very hungry,"
sighs Bear.

"The problem," says my sister, "is that Bear cannot tell time!"

"Well," says Dad, "we have all weekend to teach him."

SATURDAY

Everybody is ready.
It's time for
the lesson.

Let's start. What have I drawn here?

A pizza?

Why not?
With this little knife (also called the *hour hand*)
I cut the pizza into 12 equal slices.
Why?

**Four slices for
you, the rest
for me?**

No! Because there are 12 hours in
half a day. Each slice equals 1 hour.
Are you following me?

Hmm . . .

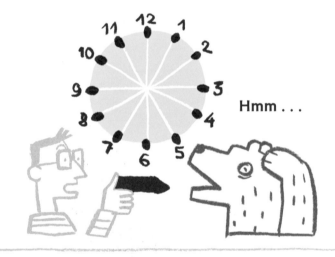

My hour hand goes around the pizza in 12 hours.
For a whole day, which has 24 hours, you need
two circuits of the pizza.

Great!

To know what time it is, all you have to do is
count the slices from the top of the pizza to
the place indicated by the hour hand.
Here, 1, 2, 3. It is . . .

Erm . . .
3 slices?

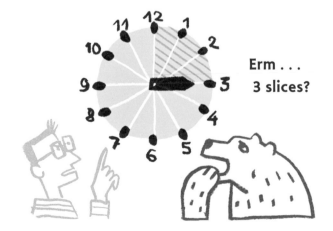

Well, 3 o'clock. Now, a little more complicated: I move the hour hand forward a little. It is . . .

3 slices
and . . . er
. . . a little bite?

Exactly! And to measure this little bite, I need another hand, longer and faster. The *minute hand*!

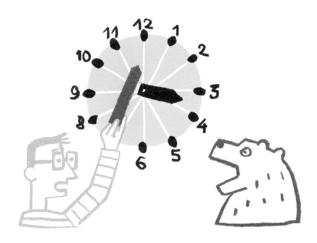

The minute hand runs around the pizza in 1 hour. I divide each of the 12 slices into 5 small pieces.
12 × 5 = 60. There are 60 minutes in 1 hour!

Those pieces are small!

Count the slices between the top of the pizza and the big hand to find out how many minutes to add to the hour indicated by the small hand. Each slice is 5 minutes . . .
5 + 5 + 5 + 5 = 20 minutes.
So the time is . . . ?

Time to eat the pizza?

No . . .
. . . time to go to bed!

SUNDAY,

Time to try again.

Let's start.
The small hand goes around in . . .

Erm . . . twelve hours!

Well done!
And twelve on the clock can mean noon, or midnight.
Noon in the daytime.
Midnight at night.

OK!

So now, it is . . . ?

Nine in the evening!

Good! You can also say, 9 p.m.

Unbelievable! He's a changed bear!

Tougher now, what time is it?

Six hours and a little more.

And we need to measure this "little more." That's why we have . . .

The big minute hand!

Bear is a genius!

Exactly! The big minute hand goes around the clock in . . . ?

One hour . . . 60 minutes!

So to know the number of minutes, you just have to add up the five-minute slices between the top of the clock and the minute hand. Here?

5 + 5 + 5 = 15. It is 6:15!

Bravo! You can tell time. Now, a little trickier . . .

. . . 35
. . . 40
. . . 45 plus, erm, 2 minutes: 10:47!

Fantastic! And here?

Noon! Time for pizza!

Wow!

On Monday, he's a new bear.
Hours and minutes no longer hold any secrets.

"Sorry! I started without you."

Once he's had his breakfast,
Bear leaves for school,
singing like a bird.

No more bubble baths.
He takes a shower on his way.

Surprise!

Time is on Bear's side now.
In a month, he has caught up.
Math, reading, writing . . . he's top of the class.

That means always
being on time.

Hurray for
punctuality!

To congratulate him,
Dad gives Bear a watch
and Mom gives him a
beautiful agenda.

MONDAY

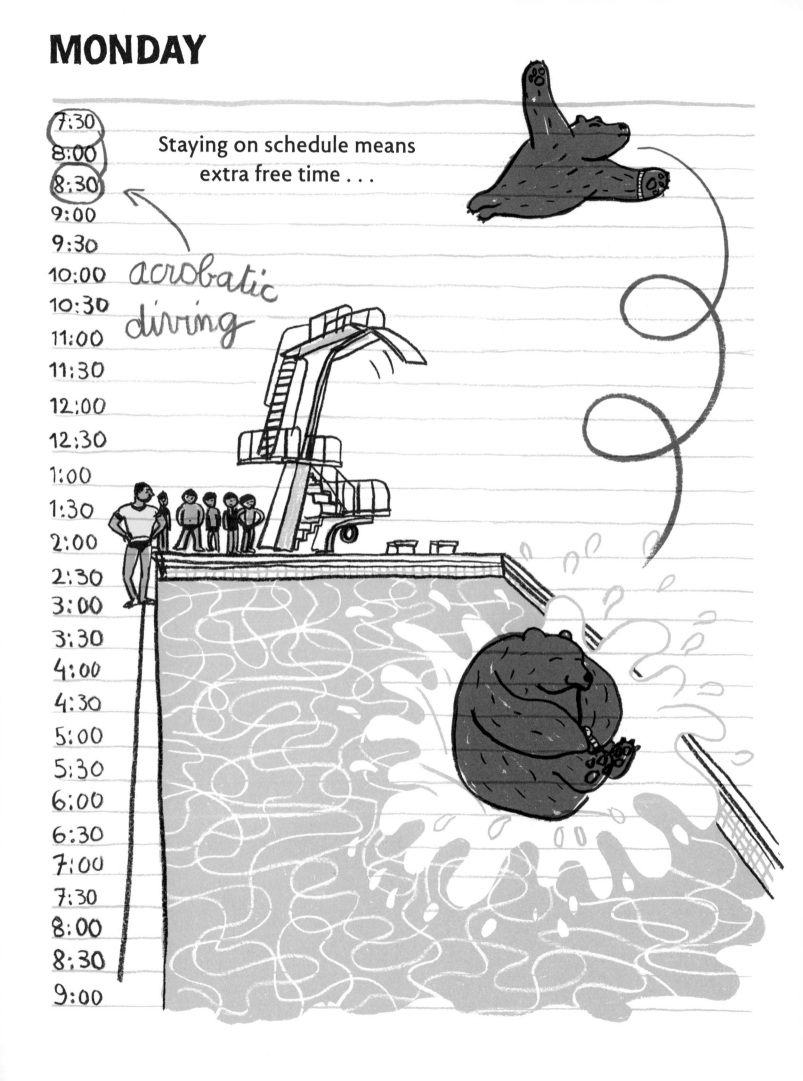

Staying on schedule means extra free time . . .

acrobatic diving

7:30
8:00
8:30
9:00
9:30
10:00
10:30
11:00
11:30
12:00
12:30
1:00
1:30
2:00
2:30
3:00
3:30
4:00
4:30
5:00
5:30
6:00
6:30
7:00
7:30
8:00
8:30
9:00

← *dance class*

. . . and Bear has organized a whole lot of extracurricular activities.

circus

class

WEDNESDAY

7:30
8:00
8:30
9:00
9:30
10:00
10:30
11:00
11:30
12:00
12:30
1:00
1:30
2:00
2:30
3:00
3:30
4:00
4:30
5:00
5:30
6:00
6:30
7:00
7:30
8:00
8:30
9:00

hockey practice

badminton

celtic harp

7:30
8:00
8:30
9:00
9:30
10:00
10:30
11:00
11:30
12:00
12:30
1:00
1:30
2:00
2:30
3:00
3:30
4:00
4:30
5:00
5:30
6:00
6:30
7:00
7:30
8:00
8:30
9:00

tuba lesson

tap dancing

art class

baking class

FRIDAY

Bear is always on the run.

SUNDAY

Until one Sunday, after many busy weeks, poor Bear collapses in a heap of flyers.

Burnout,
says the doctor.
He's gonna need some rest.

Rest, Bear!
Just naps, and mountain air.

You'll feel better.

One day, you'll go for a walk,
and that's when you'll meet . . .

. . . a beautiful bear who doesn't wear a watch!

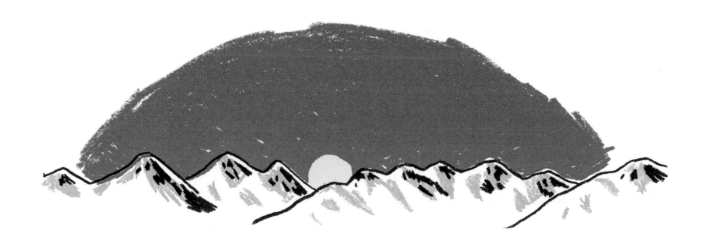

For bears, just like for people, happiness is taking
your time and listening to your heartbeat.

Hours will go by.

Days and months, too.

Time flies.

And then, one beautiful morning . . .

Guess who?